In the Beginning

In the Beginning
Moonlighting in Paris
City by the Bay
Bite the Big Apple
Caribbean Heat
Return to the Bay
Prison of the Past
Baby Girl Box Set – books 1-4

Elle Klass

Copyright © 2013 by Elle Klass
Published 2020 Books by Elle, Inc.
ISBN: 978-1-951017-12-5
All rights reserved
Editors: Dawn Lewis
Cover art created by Manuela Cardiga
For more information go to
https://elleklass.weebly.com

Books by Elle, Inc.
225 College Dr. #65504
Orange Park, FL 32065
Booksbyelle10@gmail.com

Author's Disclaimer

This book is entirely fictional. Any characters, places or events are purely figments of the author's imagination. No part of this publication may be reproduced, transmitted or redistributed either in its entirety or in part without the author's express written consent.

In the Beginning

Other Young Adult Books by Elle Klass

St. Augustine Novellas
Bloodseeker Series
Book 1 The Vampires Next Door
Book 2 The Monster Upstairs
Book 3 The Ghost Within

hidden journals
Isandro

Zombie Girl
Book 1 Premonition
Book 2 Infection
Book 3 Retribution

In the Beginning

Mom

My family wasn't the same as most. We didn't go many places or have any special "family get-togethers". In fact, everything I knew of my family was my mom. I didn't have a father or siblings - not even aunts, uncles or cousins, just me and my mother. She had long, wavy, strawberry blond hair that stretched down the length of her back. Most days she wore it on top of her head in a ponytail. She had deep brown eyes and skin the color of white bread and covered in freckles. She stood five feet tall with a frame as thin as a stop signpost. We looked nothing alike as my straight hair was the color of dark chocolate, my eyes green, and my skin four shades darker. I assumed my appearance took more after my father, whoever he was. She always appeared nervous or scared and chewed at her ragged nails. The curtains stayed drawn and when a car drove by, she peeked out and made me duck. A haze filled the cabin, caused by her chain smoking.

When I was a baby, she spent the majority of her time at home. Every once in a while, she left for two to three days then came back. Upon her return she always brought food and new clothes for me. While home she spent most of her time in her room with the door locked. The moments we spent together we played simple games or sometimes she took me to the public library where we checked out books, which she read out loud. Most of them I didn't understand, but sometimes she checked out a book for me with lots of pictures. Once a year she took me to get my picture taken by a photographer and she dressed me in stunning, expensive dresses. As I grew older, she spent less time at home. More and more often, she disappeared for days, and then for weeks. One day, after my twelfth birthday, she vanished for months.

Our home was a small shack in the outskirts of town, nestled in the woods and surrounded by overgrown foliage. The shack had three rooms. My mother's bedroom, the bathroom, and the big room. The big room contained an olive-green couch, with rips on the seat and tears in the seams that doubled as my bed. On the opposite side of the room sat a small wooden table with two chairs. The kitchen contained a stove, a sink, and a small refrigerator. Stationed above the sink hung a row of two cabinets and over the stove were another two cabinets. Bare wood floors covered every room in the shack and cold air seeped up from underneath them in the winter. A small wood-burning stove sat against the wall. During the winter she kept a fire burning. The bathroom included a tub with no shower, and a sink and toilet. A mirror with a long zig zag crack dangled above the sink, and the linoleum floor discolored from leaking water. I never went into my mother's room as she forbade it.

We didn't have luxuries such as television, cable, or a telephone. On occasion we listened to my mother's small radio. It received three stations and on good reception days, four. After my mother left for months, we lost electricity. The norm became freezing baths. My food supply ran thinner than usual and I lived off crackers and canned food items.

We lived in an average small town comprised of a few fast food joints, banks, a couple nice restaurants, a library, a park, and a few other businesses. There were three elementary schools, one junior high and one high school. I went to Brennan Elementary. I caught the bus every morning and rode it home every afternoon. If I missed the bus walking became my method of transportation. I lacked real friends in school, just a few acquaintances, and occasionally I went to birthday parties. I knew pity was the motivation behind my invitation. My shabby clothes and worn out shoes made my poverty obvious. It amazed me how other people lived. Their houses were many times the size of mine with televisions in every room and food filling the cabinets. Their families consisted of moms, dads and brothers and/or sisters - normal, happy lives. My mother and I lived a solemn life. She spent the majority of her time in her room squashing any conversation between us unless it happened through the closed door. We rationed our food. I didn't understand why our life was so different than others'.

After my mother disappeared for months, I learned to fend for myself. My mother never really took care of me; although, she had been there most of the time and brought food and clothes. I became afraid of what might happen to me if anyone knew, so I isolated myself more than usual. I came home at once from school, napped and then went trashcan diving looking for scraps of food, stale crackers, or outdated cans people threw away. It wasn't difficult to memorize the trash schedule. At home I washed my clothes in frigid water afterwards hanging them on the trees to dry. My baths comprised of frigid water with no soap or shampoo unless luck went my way and I found them in the trash. When notes needed to be signed at school, I forged her signature for everyone. In the past I did it on rare occasions out of necessity.

To entertain myself on weekends before trashcan diving, I went to the public library and checked out books and read. I pictured myself as the characters in the stories, which helped me escape the life I lived.

One Saturday afternoon I picked the lock to my mom's room and ventured inside it. I was mad at her for being gone so long and not bringing me food. In her room was a small bed which angered me as I slept on the couch with springs in my back. There was a dresser containing pictures of me and bunches of letters from people I'd never met. Needles, rubber bands, empty tubes and bags covered with a powdery residue spilled across the drawers. A bit of the residue stuck to my fingers. I licked it off, worst mistake I could have made. Ewww! After several glasses of water, the nasty chemical taste remained. I took the letters and pictures of myself, emptied out my school backpack, and stuffed them inside, along with clothes and useful trinkets I accumulated from the trash. I left in the night.

The Big City

Once I reached the edge of town I sat and waited for the freight train. Darkness settled, and fog rolled over the land. I hunkered beside a rusted-out caboose. My senses alerted to a rustling noise in the grass and my head bolted towards it. My heart skipped a few beats before an alley cat ran across the tracks. Relaxing, I heard the train pulsing through the night. It would make its usual stop, I'd hop on, whatever the destination. The driver and crew none the wiser that I was taking up car space.

As the slow purring train passed, I grabbed hold of a side rail, and wielding every bit of my strength, threw myself onto it. I took a minute to catch my breath and make sure my parts were still present. A slight sting festered at my heart for leaving the only home I'd ever known. Through the night at a steady speed the train roared forward. I curled up in a small space I found inside a car.

The next morning, not waiting for the train to make a complete stop, I hurled myself out of the car taking great care to land on my backpack and not on any precious body parts. I dusted myself off and walked until a city emerged. It was huge with people and cars everywhere. In awe I wandered around, marveling at the shiny mirrored windows of the many giant buildings. My eyes told me I blended in with everybody else. Other children were out, in pairs or small groups. My curiosity took control, and I slipped inside one of the towering buildings, a hotel. The lobby was huge and overwhelming. Scenic pictures and varieties of floral arrangements cascaded the space and aromas filled my senses. Fluffy chairs and couches dotted the rooms and small shops and restaurants filled the gaps. I found an out of the way couch, laid my head on a puffy pillow and relaxed. My body melted into the plushness and gave way to sleep.

A plump white-haired lady nudged me awake. "Excuse me, this room is closed now, can I help you find your family?"

My family? I didn't have one, but I didn't dare tell her that, so as polite and gracious I could muster said, "No thank you.

I know which room we're staying in." Quick as a landslide I left walking towards the elevators. Her eyes lingered on my back but I didn't dare look. I clicked the button and waited. With a slight hum and a whoosh, the doors opened. This was my first experience in an elevator before and even though it looked much less dangerous than jumping the train I was still nervous. As the doors opened, they gave way to a magical hall. My feet sunk in the deep carpet as if walking on pillows. A few carts filled with food waited outside rooms. It shocked me that people wasted and threw away good food. Since I hadn't eaten in a long time, I ate a few bites and stuffed more into my pack for later. The food scraps covered trays outside their rooms I was sure it wouldn't be missed.

I headed back towards the elevator to discover the rest of the hotel and rode to the top. When the doors opened a single room appeared. How strange! One room filling an entire floor. It was several times larger than the shack. When the elevator doors opened again, I stumbled in and headed downstairs, but not to the lobby, as the white-haired lady may still be lingering. Instead, I stopped on the third floor to avoid being caught and took the stairs the rest of the way. I snuck out of the hotel unnoticed and continued walking. The sleep and food renewed my energy. I took a risk, but the hotel had been a gold mine.

Night blanketed the sky reminding me I didn't yet know my territory. In Brennan I knew every inch of the terrain day or night, now I was in a new land and scared. The noise from a trashcan lid falling to the ground with a loud boom made me jump and fall into a set of stairs. I scrambled under them for shelter until morning. It wasn't the most comfortable spot on the planet, but I didn't care, people couldn't see me. When the sun came out, so did I, taking caution that no people were watching.

I took a few bites of my small food stash and realized finding more was my top priority. Better sleeping arrangements was next on the list. One night spent beneath steps hadn't been horrible but I needed something else, a place to call home. I found that home in a park- a mere coincidence. I spent the entire day milling through alley ways and the bottom floors of business and apartment buildings reaching my wit's end for the day I plopped my weary bottom onto a park bench. From the corner of my eye I spotted a horseshoe shaped walking bridge, a couple strolled across it holding hands, underneath it appeared black. Upon closer inspection a small stream ran beneath it. I crawled between the stream and the brick. Inside it was large, covered, insulated, and hidden.

The following morning, I found the restrooms and took care of business, my mind pondering the hot water in the park restrooms unlike the shack. The trail filled with twists and turns, dense foliage curved along the edges. Two young men dressed in uniform, one tall and thin, the other a few inches shorter with a medium sized build walked up the trail from the gate. Tall and thin swinging his keys in an upward fashion said, "Pork chops and rice. It was delicious!" Without hesitation I dropped and hid behind the thick shrubbery.

The shorter man responded, "When you marrying this girl?" Engrossed in their conversation they didn't notice me so I crawled across the ground and up to the curvy trail until I could no longer see them.

I named this part of town *fancy* and it offered me the most. I graduated from trashcan diving to dumpster diving. Rich people threw away the oddest things. I found a pair of good men's leather shoes and traded in my canvas ones. They fit two sizes big, but it didn't matter because they didn't have holes and the soles weren't flapping. I found a cell phone and an mp3 player. Sometimes I found TVs, radios, vacuum cleaners, clocks, and other large items. A couple of pawn shops on the other side of town didn't ask questions, so I sold the smaller items I found and left the big ones. If I found something I thought had value, I took it. On most occasions I made a few dollars, but once I got twenty dollars for an old radio in a wooden case!

I worked out a routine. In the mornings I cleaned up in the park restroom. After, I searched the city for treasures to sell and food scraps. The expensive restaurants offered the best food as they threw out meals no one ate or were missing one or two bites! I never tasted such delicious food in my twelve-year-old life. I felt healthier than I ever.

My backpack made me obvious, so I learned to hide it under the bridge in my makeshift home beneath a pile of leaves. Every day when leaving I double checked to make sure not a thing under the bridge appeared out of place as the maintenance

guys might notice. I didn't want them to
find the bag, or worse - me. Aside from that
I considered myself to be doing well.

Family

When fall hit the kids went back to school, and I no longer fit in with the crowd. The time for me to move had come, living in a park under the bridge in the *fancy* lost its practicality. I knew the day would come when I'd have to leave, so I spent August staking out other areas of town. A variety of warehouses and abandoned buildings scattered the lower end, one in particular caught my eye. I snuck inside the large empty warehouse through a window. While exploring, I found loose bricks in the wall, so I knocked out more until I could crawl inside it. Once inside, it was perfect! My body fit with room to spare. The main door was in my line of view but I couldn't be seen. I turned on my flashlight found during a dumpster diving excursion and read yesterday's newspaper. I found it on my way to the warehouse. Newspapers were easy to get hold of and I enjoyed reading; it kept me busy.

I went out at night now to do my shopping for food and pawnshop items. This side of town offered little in terms of finding items worth value. There were fast food places galore, so I lived off greasy cold hamburgers and stale, salty fries. Sometimes I got lucky and found a shake to go with them. Most days I just sucked down diluted sodas. I became familiar with the bus schedules and fare was cheap, so I ventured to other areas of the city and looked for items of value to sell and make money. Any money I made I put into the bottom of my shoes. I never parted or went anywhere without it.

Behind the goodwill I found two pillows and a huge puffy blanket I used to make myself a bed. It was difficult sneaking them back, and I didn't go unnoticed. A bum spotted me from his box, and grabbed hold of a corner of the blanket and said, "Where you going with that little girl? I think I'd like to keep it." I kicked his face hard making contact with his nose which jutted out from his sunken cheeks and ran not turning my head to look behind me until I reached the warehouse. He didn't follow me and I'm ninety nine percent sure he nursed a broken nose. A lesson taught to him so he'd leave the next little girl alone.

The bathroom in the warehouse had running water, cold water, but at least it had water. I cleaned up and washed my clothes in the sink and hung them to dry. My wardrobe consisted of two outfits while one dried I wore the other. During the day, I slept in my hidden room within the warehouse in my makeshift bed. Life wasn't horrible, but it wasn't the *fancy.*

One evening, when readying to leave, the faint sound of voices tickled my eardrums. My body went stiff as I listened. The voices grew louder. I had to make a choice: my wall home or food? I chose the safety and my wall home. Nobody would find me. I didn't like people intruding in my space and worried I would have to find a new home. With great intent I listened, attempting to eavesdrop on their conversation, but their words were too distant and blocked by the solid walls of the building.

The door burst open, and they came into my view - a girl and two boys. The girl looked thirteen and my height with shoulder length deep ginger hair that stuck out in wild ringlets encircling her face, and large round dark eyes. One boy was young - nine or ten. His curly ginger colored hair matched the girl's and his eyes were similar to hers in shape and size. I assumed they must be related. The other boy I pegged at fifteen or sixteen. He wore his straight blond hair slicked into a short ponytail that stuck out like a short feather duster. The group discussed food, and I passed bags to each other. Laughter sprung up around them and after they ate, the oldest boy made a fire in an empty metal trash can. They called him Einstein; the younger boy they called Peewee; and the girl was Star. I watched them for a while, and when the sound of snoring grew loud, I made my getaway. I tiptoed downstairs past them. Peewee rolled over on his side and opened his eyes as I slipped out the window.

My stomach growled in familiar hunger pains but I found little food that night. I got a late start because of the kids who invaded my space, and ended up settling for a cold, greasy, cheesy hamburger and a half-eaten piece of cherry pie. Thoughts of the kids encroaching in my space upset me and I hoped they'd be gone when I returned.

I knew my warehouse well and came back through a different window I considered my emergency backup. I skulked quietly to the staircase and eavesdropped on their conversation. "How much is left?" asked Einstein.

"I have three dollars and twenty-nine cents. Peewee has this broken chain he found yesterday," answered Star. Uhgg… the kids hadn't gone away, which meant I'd be caught attempting to go up the stairs. I crunched into a shadowy corner and quiet as a butterfly listened to their discussions. They were homeless waifs too and invaded my makeshift home for the night. The girl and younger boy were naïve I assumed they hadn't been on the streets long. The older boy I presumed spent more time on the streets.

"Today we will hit the train station and play it out same as we did the market," declared Einstein. A commotion followed his order as they collected themselves and left. I sighed, relieved, and I dragged myself upstairs to my makeshift bed.

By evening, the smell of cooked food wafted through the air and into my cubby which awoke me and forced my stomach to growl in hunger. They were back. I listened for a while, attempting to gain the courage to introduce myself. I lived a solitude life, no friends, no family. When my stomach and wishes for friendship reached their greatest, I mustered up the nerve to present myself, it didn't happen the way I planned in my mind. I reached the bottom step and tripped, falling flat on my face. They scattered like roaches, except the older one. Offering me his hand, he helped me to my feet.

"You OK?"

"Sure, yeah, thanks." My face must have blushed several shades of red. I jump in and out of windows and trains, yet I tripped on a step.

"I'm Einstein, and you are…"

"Uhh… I don't have a name." I stammered. Still recovering from my embarrassing fall, I couldn't fabricate a clever name for myself to give him. My real name was out of the question.

His lips turned up in a quizzical smile, his eyes rolled upwards as if deep in meditation, and he chuckled. "I get it, you don't want to give me your real name. We don't go by our real names. We have nicknames. My parents didn't name me Einstein at birth."

I giggled but remained speechless while he placed his hand under his chin, twisted his lips and scanned me with his bright eyes.

"You look like Cleopatra. Cleo, that fits you."

"Yeah, OK. I like it." I muttered deliberating on the name. In school I remembered learning something about her being the queen of Egypt. A royal name, it worked, and maybe I was the queen of this warehouse. Inwardly I chuckled at the thought.

The youngest boy and the girl came out of hiding and introduced themselves. Peewee approached me with a hotdog on a stick and offered, "We have extra." The silence and awkwardness now broken.

"Thanks, I'm starving." I wasted no time taking the hotdog from Peewee. A fire glowed in the trashcan and they roasted hotdogs over it and they had buns.

While we ate, I discovered Star and Peewee were brother and sister.

"How did you meet?" I inquired.

Einstein cleared his throat and glanced towards Star and Peewee. They met his glance as if giving him their seal of approval. "I'd had good day and was celebrating with a hearty meal at Harry's Pies. They make every flavor of pie; apple, coconut, key lime, chocolate fudge brownie... I ordered a hamburger blitz. I followed it up with a slice of apple pie and a scoop of vanilla ice cream on the side. It was good! My belly full, I left and headed back to the docks. I rounded a corner and heard muffled talking. When I looked toward the voices, I saw these two huddled in a corner." He pointed at Star and Peewee. "I couldn't leave them there and neither would tell me where they lived, so I brought them back to the docks with me."

The room fell silent and my mind searched for the words to ask my question. Two young children, Star my age and Peewee a couple years younger not fit to be alone on the streets, alone in an alley, why were they there? I deliberated for a few seconds and decided to tell my story, then maybe they would share theirs. "I left home a few months ago when my mom disappeared. What about your parents?" There, I asked, and expected no more of an explanation than what I gave. Star opened her mouth to speak then looked at Peewee who stared at her with huge, blank, round eyes.

After a sigh she stated, "We don't have any. They died when Peewee was a baby. I barely remember them." She stole a glance at Einstein who sat quiet. "We've bounced around from one foster home to the next and the last place, the dad was crazy. We left."

Their lives had been as fraught with torture as mine I found that to be comforting.

Einstein broke the silence this time. "Since we are confessing, I guess it's my turn. I left home several months ago when, I, uh, we, my parents and I, didn't get along so well." None of us asked anymore questions that involved our past lives. Stashed in a closet was the best place for them.

Over the next few days, we got acquainted with each other and I understood why they called the older boy Einstein. He was smart and assigned us jobs, such as collecting food or small items we needed such as jewelry or electronics, anything we could use to make a few bucks. Day to day we never knew what types of trinkets and treasures people would throw out waiting for us to find. He even taught us how to work in pairs and pickpocket unsuspecting people to steal items we later sold. He worked on this with Star and Peewee, but to me it was new.

"You're a quick study." He told me after we teamed up to snatch a man's wallet. The man took it out of his pocket to remove his credit card, setting the wallet on the counter as he swiped. I tripped and fell into him and Einstein slipped the wallet into his own pocket while the man helped me up and asked if I was OK. I thanked him and proceeded out the door. The wallet contained eighty-three dollars which we kept and tossed the wallet into a dumpster. The money served in feeding us well and I felt like part of a family complete with brothers and a sister. Yet, as much as I liked them and trusted them, I never showed any of them my secret place and I was near positive they'd never find it - *my* safe place.

Approaching Winter

We burned stray wood and paper in the trashcan for warmth, and stock-piled blankets, coats and extra clothes during the frigid winter months. Star and Peewee huddled together for warmth and Einstein held me close. The city was marvelous and bustling with life making it easy now to fit into a crowd and earn extra money. We tricked people out of hundreds of dollars in cash taking advantage of their generosity.

Einstein found an old small plastic Christmas tree in a dumpster and brought it to the warehouse. He insisted it wasn't Christmas without presents so we found gifts for each other and placed them under the tree. It was the first Christmas in my life I celebrated. My mother never celebrated any holiday, nor did I ever receive gifts on special occasions such as my birthday. My mom's gift every year was an expressionless 'Happy birthday'. I found a working gold watch with engraving on the underside of the face plate, but that didn't matter. I gave it to Einstein because of his preoccupation with keeping track of time. Star found and gave Peewee a new pair of shoes as his were falling apart at the seams and unsuitable for trudging through piles of snow. Star gave me a fiction book as I loved to read, and Einstein gave Star a tiara because she adored anything with sparkles and glitter. Instead of eating leftovers or cooking canned meats or hotdogs, we took our money and ate inside a nice restaurant. We splurged and partied creating an unforgettable Christmas.

Einstein survived on his own longer than the rest of us and wanted more than dumpster leftovers and abandoned warehouses. He grew eager to leave and developed a plan to heist jewelry and small valuable items from people's homes while they were away on vacation. Later we'd sell everything for cash.

We became obsessed with staking out neighborhoods and houses. The four of us wanted the same thing, a "normal" life. We found homes spaced apart geographically, hoping to draw less attention than if we hit homes in the same areas. Einstein and I hit the first home and everything went smooth as melted caramel. We chose the house after observing the owner's leaving the spare key hidden under a stone behind the house. The ordinary neighborhood and tract homes meant no alarms. For our first heist we made a wise choice.

Once inside the house we used our flashlights to find our way around, careful not to shine them towards the windows and take the chance of alerting the neighbors. In the master bedroom we found a solid gold chain, two gold rings with precious stones that Einstein said were amethyst, emeralds, and onyx but mostly costume stuff. How Einstein knew each stone stumped me. In the dining hutch we found crystal goblets. Einstein claimed they were real crystal because he wet his finger, swirled it around the top of one glass and made it sing. A cool trick I wouldn't have known on my own. I took his knowledge of precious stones and crystal as clues to his upbringing and guessed he'd lived a more privileged life than myself.

"How did you know to do that?"

The corners of his lips turned upward in a smile. "I can't tell you all my secrets."

We wrapped the goblets in dish towels using great care and placed them into our backpacks.

After Einstein and I successfully hit a few homes, Star decided she wanted in on the scam. Einstein thought it was a bad idea because of Peewee, but Star insisted. She wanted a piece of the action. She and Einstein butted heads over it causing friction amongst us.

One night Star and Peewee followed us out and caught up to us as we finished hijacking items from the house. The second we stepped outside the house a familiar whisper, "Cleo" alerted me Star followed us. My body halted mid-stride as I caught sight of her and Peewee's shadows standing against the wall of the house. Einstein motioned for them to edge their way to the back of the house where there were no light sensors. Star shuffled towards us, but Peewee stepped out too far and the lights went on brightening the entire side of the house. Oh crap! We fled in varying directions. I held the bag of loot in my hand and once I ran I didn't turn my head to look behind me. I hastened my pace at the sounds of people. Several blocks away I cowered in an alley to catch my breath.

Einstein was right behind me and ducked into the alley with me.

"Star and Peewee, are they with you?"

He shook his head as if to say 'no' and turned his eyes downward. "It's time to leave" he said after a moment of silence.

"OK, yeah, we need to get back."

He grasped my shoulders. "Leave - as in this city. There were too many lights, commotion, and sirens at the scene for Star and Peewee to slip away. They aren't as savvy as we are. The police are gonna be looking for us next."

My mind absorbed with escaping I missed the wailing sirens. He was right and my head reeled at the implications his words threw at me.

"You think they'll tell on us?"

The nod of his head told me 'yes'.

I couldn't leave yet I needed my bag from its secret place.

"We gotta go back to the warehouse. I have something hidden there that I need." His eyes grew soft, and he agreed.

Back at the warehouse, I went straight to my secret place. Within minutes the sound of voices tickled our eardrums and lights flashing beneath us.

"Squish in beside me."

Without a moment to spare Einstein squeezed in the cubby hole. Radios blared on the other side of the cubby and police scoured the building but came up empty. I whispered in Einstein's ear, "Star and Peewee squealed quick."

"They did - or the police are here for something else." 'Something else' was possible. Either way, neither of us wanted to get caught. Hours passed with Einstein and I scrunched on top of each other. Teenage hormones, close quarters, and our semi attraction to each other brought our relationship to a new level. Our hearts raced together from the excitement. Einstein held me flush against him.

"I love you Cleo."

The sound of his words caused a wave of want to wash came over me and I kissed him. My first kiss ever. I drove my tongue deep inside his mouth. Einstein's words and kiss melted my heart. My own mother never showed me any affection. As I kissed him, he kissed me back. We explored under each other's clothes. Our fingers and hands discovering the joys of the opposite sex. I yearned for his love and firm embrace. The moment sent thrilled me, I didn't want it to end.

The next day we waited for Star and Peewee, but we both knew the police found them. Under the cover of dusk we snuck out, taking great pains to not get caught.

An Alternative

The bus station was several miles away and creeping in the shadows along the alley ways was taking too long. A gas station with flickering lights was ahead and a brilliant idea flashed through my brain.

I pointed towards a truck parked at a gas pump. "Look, maybe we can jump into the back of that truck and catch a ride."

Einstein stopped and observed, curling his lips as he thought a minute. "If he goes inside, we can make it, but we'll be exposed for a couple minutes."

"We aren't exactly in the good side of town. Do you think people are gonna care about two kids running across the street?"

"OK, follow me." He slipped across the street. I waited for his OK and followed him to where he waited beside a dumpster.

"What are they dumping in their trash?" I asked with one finger over my nose as the trash inside wreaked of a rotting dead body. Einstein shifted his eyes my way and placed his finger over his mouth stifling a laugh. The man finished pumping his gas, climbed into his truck and drove away.

We stayed in position and waited for another vehicle. Several cars later, and the second we were getting ready to move on, another truck rolled into the station. It was old and sported a patchy paint job, along with several spots of rust. We looked at each other, knowing this was the one.

"I will distract him; you jump in the back."

"Cleo, what…"

I didn't wait for him to finish and wasn't walking the entire way. I pulled down my shirt enough to show my blossoming boobs and walked past the man at the pump dropping a trinket from my pocket. Next, I leaned over and wiggled my butt in his direction to pick it up and walked inside the store. He took the bait following me inside the store a few minutes later. My head start enabled me to sneak through the tall stocked shelves to the back and slip outside the door. I ran around the front to the truck and leaped into the bed where Einstein waited for me.

"Smooth. Lucky for us he's a pedophile." Einstein barked, half annoyed and half laughing.

I smiled out of sheer satisfaction. "You bet." We lay flat and motionless against the bottom of the truck bed.

A few minutes later we heard the driver approach, mumbling under his breath, "Why do I chase cute young ass? Untouched meat."

He got into the truck and it started with a sputter and cough before it jerked forward.

Together

The city lights dwindled into sparse street lights and trees. My lungs filled with exhaust fumes, and my body felt as though a jack hammer pounded it into a pulp. The truck slowed, turned and abruptly stopped, our heads slamming into the back of the cab.

The door creaked open and a heavy foot hit the ground then another, his footsteps cumbersome along the pavement. Next, they halted and lumbered their way back. With the truck bed so junky we had nowhere to move. We looked at each other and then at the huge hairy hand that forced its way over the truck bed, we both jumped out and ran. "What the fu…" He called, but we scurried into the woods surrounding his house. I rested myself against a tree to catch my breath. The prickles in my side bore the illusion that a thousand knives were poking into it. Einstein fell to the ground, both of us panting.

"This is eerie… hmm… What is it that happens to teens alone in the woods?" Einstein asked widening his eyes into basins of fear.

"Nothing more than teens alone in the city with many types of nutcases."

"Really, haven't you ever been to the movies?" A look of curiosity flashed across his face.

"No, never." The sadness in my own voice resonating inside me.

"There is always a crazy stalker with a machete or chain saw waiting to chop up innocent teens." Einstein declared, still wearing his fear face.

"I grew up in a place like this, the woods surrounding me. I was more scared alone in the city with so many people until I found you. It was creepy, and I kept myself hidden at night." I allowed my body to crumple next to his, we lay on the forest floor, his arms around my waist.

As the morning sun peaked, we continued our journey to the nearest town. Neither of us had any idea where to find the road, so we kept on a straight path through the woods. Birds chirped and squirrels chattered in the trees. We followed a stream we found.

"Hold still, I hear something," whispered Einstein.

Keeping still with our ears open, we both heard a loud chink-chink sound. He grabbed my waist, pushed me behind him and we crouch walked behind a bush. The heavy footsteps pounded the forest floor until they were on top of us. We peered through the bush and saw him, the same man in whose truck we hitched a ride. He carried a shotgun in his hands. We sat still as the hundred-year-old redwoods we hid behind until he turned and left.

My heart slowed inside my chest. He turned back suddenly, and in an instant, raised his gun and shot through the bush. The pellet whizzed past my forehead. Quick as lightning, I jumped to my feet and headed anywhere but there. I heard Einstein behind me and the man's heavy footsteps followed in pace. I ran through brush, jumped over hundred-year-old tree roots, my legs gaining agility as I jetted through the woods. Another chink-chink sound followed by a shot deafened the forest, but it wasn't even close. My body took on a flight of its own, stopping when I got to the road.

I looked and Einstein was beside me his long legs in stride with my short ones. A few cars buzzed past us honking their horns and the man stomped back into the forest, defeated. We made it to the other side of the road after playing chicken with the traffic.

A car pulled over beside us. The people inside the car, a middle-aged man and woman with friendly faces, rolled down the window and asked, "You kids need a ride?"

Einstein grabbed my hand and replied, "Thanks." We piled into the vehicle.

The man narrowed his eyes and inspected us. "Where you headed?"

"Back into town."

"What are you kids doing out here this early in the morning?" A hint of prying noticeable in the woman's tone.

"Camping with friends. Claire twisted her ankle and her boyfriend Jack took her into town. We figured we'd wait it out, but it's been too long." Einstein replied with a fantastic lie that eased off his tongue as if it was truth.

"In these woods? They are privately owned by Crazy Man Shaw. You must not be from around here." The words rolled off her tongue.

"We know that now."

Einstein followed up with, "We're from the city."

The couple continued to talk with us probing our minds, looking to poke holes in our story, but they got us into town and dropped us at the hospital. We thanked them, waited for them to leave and walked to a diner across the street. We ate and got directions to the bus station. Towns this small were dangerous for two runaways.

Night Creeper

We caught a bus headed into Washington state and another big city. It was easier to hide in cities, then in small towns where everyone knew everyone. Once in the city, we bought new clothes and threw away our others. There was no way to salvage them as Crazy Man Shaw truck bed yuck and exhaust covered them. We needed to blend in so it wasn't obvious we were two runaways.

Einstein took me on my first trip to a mall and a movie theater. He slipped his arm around my waist, veered me towards the movie theater and purchased two tickets to a movie called *Night Creeper.* "It's your first movie, so we have to do this right."

"Right. You mean there is a way to do it wrong?" I asked, half joking and half serious.

A cockeyed smile twisted across his face and he bought a large popcorn and slushy.

I was in awe at the size of the screen it took up an entire wall, and the sound roared from varying angles. We sat in the front row, which made it appear even larger, and I strained my neck backwards to watch the movie. We shoveled most of our popcorn into our mouths before the movie started and tossed a few kernels at one another. I gripped Einstein's hand and buried my head into his chest for most of the duration of the movie. He chose a movie involving young kids lost in a swamp with something hunting them, killing them off one at a time. It was too close for comfort since we just escaped our own nightmare in the woods. I snuggled into the crook of his arm with one eye on the screen and saved my complaints about his humor for after the movie.

"I can't believe you!" I jostled hitting him square on the arm. "Really?"

His smile shined from one end of his face to the other as he responded between laughing convulsions. "I wanted you to know," he gasped, holding his stomach as tears poured from his eyes and over his cheeks, "how lucky you were."

Not being able to stop myself, I laughed along with him. Tears flowed from my eyes too; finally, we sat regaining our composures. I slurped the last drop of slushy to wet my dry throat and threw the cup at him.

He picked up the cup and tossed it into the trash then grabbed my hand in his. "I have another surprise for my naïve girlfriend."

Girlfriend? His words made my heart swell three sizes. I gripped his hand tight, and we maneuvered our way through the crowd.

Next, he took me to a video game palace. Money was always too scarce to splurge playing video games but this day we made an exception. In wonderment my eyes scanned the blinking, flashing, and colorful lights. Sounds bustled at us from every direction. We placed one-dollar bills in a machine, and it spat out gold tokens, which went into the games, bringing them to life, whirling and beaming. Einstein was a whiz and the video games spit out tickets at him. I stunk at everything, except one game in which I threw a ball into a ring. Each ring had a point value, the center ring having the highest. I kept winning, and the machine spit out tickets. After a couple hours of playing we accumulated tickets enough to buy a camera that was so small it fit into my pocket. It came with a small SD card.

We left the arcade and made use of our camera, taking pictures of everything. Once we filled the SD card, we took it to a one-hour photo shop and had the pictures printed. I snuck a picture of a man picking his nose in a car, and another of a boy who fell off his skateboard. The skateboard continued to roll, and a woman tripped over it. Einstein got a picture of a drunk sleeping it off in an alley. We took pictures of tall mirrored buildings, an amazing three tier water fountain, and of each other with goofy faces and poses. It was the best day of my thirteen-year life and I laughed harder than ever before, my stomach still bearing the pain. Einstein erased the SD card. His tech abilities convinced me his previous life was a hundred times more privileged than mine. I pondered again why he ran away.

With our cash running low, we found a pawn shop in a questionable area of town and sold part of our jewelry. Our day one big excursion meant for fun. It was easy enough to disappear in the city, although not a place we wanted to stay. We made the choice to hit more cities and pull off more heists to finance the start of our life together.

On our way to the train station we witnessed a horrific crime that I got on camera. The pawn shop was in a crummy part of town. There were hookers on street corners and groups of people together talking, arguing and making drug deals. We walked past them, holding each other's hands for dear life and not saying a word or looking too hard at what they were doing. A few people made comments to us, but nobody stopped or harassed us. In the past I witnessed homeless kids get beaten and tortured by street people and forced to hang with street scum for protection. I imagined most of the kids were, homeless and without families.

The sun crept downwards, giving into dusk. The drug dealers, hookers, and general low life scum became less and less as we continued our walk to the train station.

We overheard two men arguing. Without a half second of hesitation and on instinct we both stopped and ducked behind a car to avoid being noticed. My eyes darted across the street to the train station a few paces away. I considered my chances and figured it best to stay put, at least for the moment. The longer we stayed hidden the less chance we had of getting hurt. The two men argued for a while then one of them pulled a gun on the other and pushed him. Light twinkled off the barrel as he pointed it towards the other man, curse words surged from his mouth. My heart beat like a drummer on caffeine. Without thinking I took the camera from my pocket and snapped pictures.

Einstein, his brows furrowed into a V whispered, "What...? Put that away or you'll get us killed."

He was right but an urge within compelled me and my hands refused to cooperate. The pushed man, fuming with anger, pulled out a gun too and waved it in the air toward other man. His hand shook with tremors and the gun went off followed by a stream of shrapnel flowing from the barrel. The first bullet hit a streetlight then plowed straight into the head of the other man. He fell to the ground with a thunk, a chunk of his head missing and blood flowing in a steady stream.

At that moment, the flash of my camera caught the shooter's eye, and he took a poorly aimed shot in our direction.

He tossed the gun into a nearby dumpster and ran. It landed with a thud. I looked from the dumpster to the station, considering going for the gun. At that moment Einstein yanked my body from its current position, took my hand and pulled me across the street. We slipped inside the station, our hearts beating out of control inside our chests.

We rested against the wall to catch our breath and allowed our hearts to return to their normal pulse. Einstein spoke again. "What were you doing? Are you crazy?"

"I... I don't know," I responded, my head poised downwards.

He took my chin in his hand and forced it upwards until my eyes met his. "I saw your face. I watched your eyes. You were going for the gun." His eyes unwavering and burning deep into my soul.

I stammered, tears now forming in the corners of my eyes. "Yes, I... I wasn't thinking but reacting." He held me to his chest; my shoulders heaved in and out, the flood gates around my eyes giving way to a wild flow of tears. He walked me to a quiet corner where we sat, neither of us muttering a sound. Police and ambulance sirens roared outside the station. Einstein used his pointer finger and wiped my face then we disappeared on the next available train. The train hooted and began its journey to our next destination, leaving behind the most wonderful and second most, frightening day of my life.

A Close Call

Over the following months we bounced from one city to the next, blurring my memory. We changed our appearances by wearing layered clothing and hats we pulled off on the run. Our stay in each city lasted long enough for us pull off a couple heists, make money then we disappeared. We kept a low profile, ghost people, slipping in and out unnoticed.

I took the time to keep up with our crime sprees through the newspaper. The police were clueless and never linked them together. Under the small crimes section in tiny print is where I found most our thefts listed with one exception- the judge's house.

We got cocky and chose a house in a ritzy gated community belonging to a judge. Einstein posed as a landscaper replacement from a job agency with the usual crew and did inside surveillance. He staked out the judge's property and found a small gap at the bottom of the fence big enough for us to squeeze underneath without getting scratched. After we squeezed under the gap, we traipsed through the woods surrounding the inside of the gate, which backed up to his property. Einstein did his usual security system magic by cutting the outside wires and we were in the house.

The judge's house was full of valuables; diamond earrings, gold necklaces adorned with amethyst, rubies, emeralds, and onyx. We took small stuff that fit in our back packs to be carried out and pawned without drawing attention.

While in the judge's office I dug through his desk drawers and found a bundle of cash and a gold letter opener then the sirens wailed in the distance, forcing a shot of panic in my belly. Without thinking I stuffed the letter opener and cash into the bag. Einstein and I high-tailed it out of the house. The sirens howled behind us as we cut back through the woods and slid under the fence on our backs. I breathed a sigh of relief.

"That was too close."

Einstein took my hand, helping me to my feet. "No kidding." We slunk back to our temporary home and dumped our packs.

The wad of cash, jewelry, and letter opener rolled out of my backpack hitting the cement floor.

"Holy cow Cleo!" Einstein grabbed the letter opener and twisted it in his hand holding it up to the light. "Look at the engraving. We can't sell this it belonged to a famous eighteenth century author."

I lowered the wad of cash I held in my hand. "I... it was in my hand when I heard the sirens."

"It's solid gold. We'll take care of it later." He looked at the huge bundle of cash. "You want help counting?"

"Sure." I handed him half the bundle, and he stole a kiss on my lips.

The grand total of our loot for the day amounted to $5,000 in cash, five new gold chains adorning various gemstones, diamond earrings, a silver place setting, brass candleholders, and a gold letter opener engraved with an eighteenth-century authors name.

The judge offered a reward for the return of the letter opener. We thought of various scenarios in which to collect the reward, but any of them led to police involvement. Chimes went off inside my head and I came up with a brilliant plan.

We wiped the letter opener clean, even though we always wore gloves, and found a drunk homeless man passed out in an alley, derelicts littered the shabbier parts of cities. I pressed the letter opener against his fingertips and left it under his hand while Einstein used a pay phone to call it in anonymously. A tall apartment building stood kitty corner to where the derelict man lay. We chose that building to meet back up and watched the scene from the fourth-floor landing. The judge was grateful to have his letter opener back, and we took deep breaths that we pulled off framing the innocent homeless man.

A Change of Pace

The experience with the judge forced us both to evaluate our current lives, and they were becoming dangerous. We were growing paranoid, always watching our backs and keeping our heads low. My senses more acute and my body on full alert every second.

We grabbed a continental breakfast from the local Coziness Inn, a trick we learned on our travels. The management and guests never chased us out when we walked in off the streets, filled our plates and stuffed our faces. I loaded my plate with bacon, eggs, sausage, and a bagel with cream cheese and took a seat next to Einstein. He piled the food on his plate twice as high as mine with pancakes smothered in syrup, eggs, and fruit.

He swallowed a huge bite of pancake, wiped his mouth, and set his napkin on the table. "I inventoried our loot this morning and we're set."

I leaned across the table and whispered, "How much?"

He held up his hands and blinked ten fingers. Ten grand! Holy pumpkins we're rich!

"I'm tired of running and sneaking continental breakfasts. I want a hot shower and a real job. Mostly, I want a life with you." The sincerity of his words shown through his eyes.

"Me too. Any ideas where?"

He shook his head no.

"I saw a library a few blocks from here. I'll find a place you come up with our cover stories."

We fist bumped, finished our food and walked to the library. There I researched the country searching for a large enough town where we could blend in, but small enough we could make connections. I found that place in Alabama.

Einstein decided we should pose as a young married couple. He swiped simple matching gold wedding bands for us to wear completing our cover.

The sun disappeared, and the darkness lingered when we arrived in Alabama. A thick blanket of liquid filled the air causing it to look hazy. Our stomachs growled with hunger after the long ride. We found a diner, the outside worse for wear and the neon sign flashed half the letters. Inside a bar stretched long in front of the grill. Metal barstools with shiny cracked plastic seats lined the bar and booths lined the windows made with the same metal and shiny plastic as the barstools. Country rock music played quietly from a jukebox. I smelled the aromas of coffee and greasy foods. Inside my mouth the saliva built from my hunger.

A plump waitress, with a round friendly face and dirty blond hair pulled tightly into a bun with a few stray ringlets that bounced as she walked, handed us two menus. "Gimme a holla when y'all're ready." Her smile beamed from ear to ear. After a quick glance across the menu, I knew what I wanted. "Where y'all from?" she asked taking our orders.

"Seattle," said Einstein.

I smiled remembering our time in Washington and Seattle. We talked with the waitress then a forty-ish man came in and sat next to us joining the conversation. We fed them our cover story, and they told us a couple places renting rooms by the week.

One motel was close to the diner, and we were both ready to wash off in hot water and rest in an actual bed since we hadn't done either of the two together for a stretch of months.

The room we checked into contained a small kitchenette with a refrigerator, a TV, bed, dresser, closet and a table for two. Thick green curtains, stained by the sun, fell across the window. The bedspread was rubber ducky yellow with green vines laced across it.

In the bathroom a shower beckoned for me to climb in and wash the dirt off my body. Never in my life had I taken a shower. We looked at each other, stripped off our clothes, and jumped in together. I stood underneath the shower head allowing the water to pour down the length of my body. It was heaven. Not until the water turned cold did either of us get out.

Now clean we didn't want to dress back in our dirty clothes so we washed them in the bathtub and hung them to dry across the shower curtain rod. We slipped into the bed and Einstein turned on the TV using the remote. Occasionally I saw TV shows on store display models or school but never watched in bed or used a remote, TV was luxury for "normal" people. I wrapped my arm across Einstein's chest and leaned my head on his shoulder. He lifted his free arm over my head and caressed my hair until I fell asleep.

Our Life Together

I spent my days watching the TV and playing with the remote. The characters "lives" including their jobs, families, friends, and school intrigued me. I couldn't find one show that starred a character growing up in a shack with a part time mom, no other family, and exhausting every choice left at a young age. I pondered whether my mom ever came back to the shack and cried when she found it empty. If she came back to the shack, she wouldn't have shed any tears but jumped for joy to see me gone then slammed drugs into her arm in undisturbed peace. On the streets I saw plenty enough to understand she was a user and didn't doubt it was the reason for her mysterious disappearance. I theorized her mind suspended in a permanent "high" making it impossible for her to come back to reality. Either way, it didn't matter anymore. Now Einstein and I had each other.

I took up cooking to pass the time, which I learned from TV. My mother's menu consisted of cooked macaroni and cheese, hot dogs, grilled cheese or soup from a can. I hated those foods and refused to cook them, but I loved to cook! We shopped and filled our little kitchen with spices, meats, cheeses, pastas, and other real and normal foods. Einstein bought me a cookbook filled with delicious recipes for me to whip up in the kitchen. We ate fresh food - no more trash can leftovers. I discovered how to make salads, cook meats, sauté rice, bake potatoes, boil pasta, add flavorings and became a pro in no time. The aromas filled my kitchen and radiated throughout the motel. My cooking led to many a friendship there.

Our lives settled into a slow pace. Before I became a kitchen wizard, we became regulars at the diner, and they offered Einstein a legitimate job as a dish washer and fill-in cook. We were a real family and in love with each other, always showering each other with affection. The touch of his lips on mine sent shivers throughout my body and I loved the way his hands felt caressing my skin. In turn I couldn't stop touching him, rubbing my hand across his facial hair stubble, combing and styling his long, lush, thick blond channels of hair. My heart swelled for him so much I thought it might burst.

Discussions of our lives before knowing each other were taboo. The most I told him was the tidbit the day we met at the warehouse and then the night in Crazy Man Shaw's woods. I picked up on enough tidbits of information to comprehend there was a lot more to Einstein's story. In the past he lived a privileged life. However, our pasts didn't matter. The present and new memories we created are what counted.

Copy - catters

With each passing day I felt more and more "normal" and the atrocities of my past faded. At fifteen years of age my life became enjoyable and relaxed.

An older couple, Mr. and Mrs. Turner lived across the courtyard from us. He had a tall, thin build with a crown of graying hair on his head while Mrs. Turner contrasted with her round figure, short height, and thinning salt and pepper hair. They lost their home and savings when he became handicapped. She worked full time cleaning homes to support them. Sometimes, I went into the courtyard and visited with him during the day. Other days we watched cooking shows together.

Next door to us lived James a middle-aged man, average looking with a bald patch on top of his head framed by dark hair. His daughter, LulaBell a couple years younger than me was my height, with a head of full-bodied hair every bit as dark as her father's. After school she came over and we worked on her homework. Sixth grade is when my school career ended. Her education fascinated me and I soaked up everything like an absorbent paper towel. In science she learned about cells and the human body. It amazed me how every part of an organism worked together, and my education on heredity confirmed my mother and I lacked a genetic connection. She learned geography and information about the cultures of other countries. Her studies became mine and our friendship blossomed.

My vicarious learning through LulaBell's education led to an increasing Paris curiosity. I imagined Einstein and me starting fresh and not worrying one day we'd be caught and thrown in teen jail.

For Christmas with our neighbors and actual friends we planned a big feast. We worked out a menu, each of us bringing something different. I decided on baked ham and a cherry pie. James and LulaBell brought sweet potato pie and beer and the Turners brought baked apples and rolls. We had our celebration in the courtyard between our rooms. The mild Alabama weather made an outdoor celebration possible, and the courtyard contained plenty of tables and chairs. We ate and drank the night away. Like us our neighbors were good people with sketchy pasts.

After dinner and a fantastic Christmas Einstein and I settled into our bed with full bellies.

"I can't remember eating a sweeter ham." Einstein said rubbing his belly.

"That was the brown sugar I drizzled on it." I rolled onto my side to face Einstein, propping my head on my hand. His eyes shifted and met mine greeting me with love. "I've been thinking…" I wasn't sure how to break the news and disrupt out quaint life. You know I keep track of the news. Our heist at the Judge's house brought attention to our crimes. The police are searching more than ever and making connections. They haven't released any hard evidence, but they found a couple copy-catters - two kids in Oregon, a boy and a girl. They broke into a home, stole jewelry, a baseball card collection, and brass cufflinks. A neighbor saw them running from the house and called the police. They caught the kids. Their ages and brief descriptions match Star and Peewee. They lived in a foster home during the time frame we actively thieved. In time they ran away leaving newspaper clippings behind in the home. The authorities assumed the kids admired our handy work. Well duh, right?"

"Duh. The good ole days. I don't miss them and don't get crazy notions that our victims were innocent."

"What do you mean?"

"Look around you at our neighbors. Everybody has something to hide."

His words drifted through my mind for a second and dissipated as a crazy copy-catter detail entered my mind. "The house had a silent alarm and the guy that owned it was an alarm specialist and rigged his house with a remarkable system. The alarm triggered the police before the neighbor's call."

Einstein caressed my cheek and fondled my ear. "And you have an idea where we should go?"

He knew me well. "Of course! How about Paris? They are known for having the best food. The city is small but populated. It's a different country across the Atlantic. We'd be able to fit in and hide and it's full of history and legends."

"Like the catacombs beneath Paris that harbors the remains of hundreds of dead people?"

I grabbed my pillow and hit him with it. "I wasn't thinking anything that scary but yeah!"

He caught my pillow and hit me back then grabbed my waist and brought my body on top of his, planting a sensuous tongue filled kiss on my mouth. "Paris it is, but first we enjoy the rest of the holidays."

I rolled off Einstein onto my back and stared at the popcorn ceiling. "This Christmas was great wasn't it? I'll miss everyone especially James and LulaBell."

When the Past Catches Up

We spent several months vigorously planning our escape. Our slow-paced life together was taking a dramatic turn and neither of us wanted to spend the next few years in a juvenile detention center. With methodic research we developed a plan. We didn't need passports or any form of identification. We planned to jump a train headed North up the east coast to New York, and from there steal aboard a freight ship headed to France.

Zero hour was drawing close for Einstein and me. We said goodbye to our close neighbors and the diner owner and staff wanted to see us before we disappeared into the oblivion. After our evening eating greasy diner food with stuffed bellies we held hands and strolled to the motel. The night was warm and humidity hung thick in the air surrounding us. The streetlights above glowed, halos enclosed the falling light leaving no clues that a strange new twist would send me rocketing into a different world. Within seconds our life together ended abruptly, screeching tires blasted our ears, and a car veered around the corner aimed at us.

"Watch out!" Einstein pushed me and I spiraled face forward, my legs falling under me. I looked towards Einstein and screamed, "No!" The car hit him square on, throwing him several feet, and disappeared.

On my feet I ran to Einstein and lay my head on his chest. The usual rhythm of his heart ceased. His chest didn't rise and fall with air. Time froze and my heart dropped deep into my chest, sadness oozed through every pore inside my body. Inside I screamed; outside my body convulsed as rivers of loss and sudden fear coursed through my veins. My tragic life was finally whole and right, we were leaving, and within seconds his life destroyed! I couldn't panic or mourn him, I had to leave. The watch I gave him our first Christmas together twinkled on his wrist, I slid it off along with the gold band on his finger. "I love you," I whispered giving him one last kiss as tears poured from my eyes in flooding streams while my legs took hold of me. Once again, I was running, a familiar friend.

A couple blocks away, my body halted at a payphone and my fingers punched the numbers 9-1-1. My voice shook. "There has… been a hit and… run. A man… he's… he's dead." My hands jammed the receiver back on its holster and I dashed to our room. My neighbor next door, James, spied me scurrying across the street, so he came over and I let him inside the room.

James eyes shifted as he looked around the room. "Where's Einstein?"

I choked and buckets of tears streamed from my eyes. "He's dead. He's been hit I have to leave now." I threw what I could into my backpack.

He grabbed my hands. "Sit." We sat on the edge of the bed. "Don't leave yet. I can help you by providing a passport." I recognized he'd always been up to shady business transactions but never questioned it, which must be why he didn't question my urgency to leave after the sudden loss of Einstein.

Tears ran rampant over my face, and my voice quivered. "How… how long?"

"No more than forty-eight hours." James folded me into his arms as I cried on his chest. He understood we had secrets just as he did but never asked. Now he wanted to give me a legal ticket out of this country. I stayed for two more days, grieving my beloved Einstein, and reading up on his death. The authorities didn't know who hit him or made the mysterious the 911 call.

After two days, true to his word, James provided me with a passport and new identity. I was eighteen-year-old Justine Holmes instead of sixteen-year-old Cleo. I took the passport, my survival bag, a blue shirt of Einstein's that carried his scent, and boarded a plane to France. My mind retraced every precious moment I was lucky enough to share with Einstein.

Stay tuned for Cleo's next adventure…

Moonlighting in Paris
Baby Girl JJ

Justine

James and LulaBell transported me to the bus station so I could hop the bus to the airport. I thanked them and we gave each other huge hugs. I watched their truck pull away and meandered into the station.

Between the second and third stops I had a six-hour gap between busses so I explored. I found a salon within a few blocks of the station and resolved to get my hair done. The name Justine Holmes demanded class, which I had little of in my present condition. The experience was new and exhilarating. As a child my mom took household scissors when my hair grew out of control.

The beautician had deep scarlet lopsided hair; it hung longer on the left side

of her face than the right. I wanted
something more conservative, so I asked for
blond highlights throughout the top, and
underneath kept my natural chocolate. She
trimmed several inches off the back,
shaping it with long layers. She then styled
it and handed me a vanity mirror. I no
longer looked like homely, abandoned, and
poor distraught Cleo, but Justine.

To top off my new look I bought both a
pedicure and manicure. My feet and hands
were in gnarly shape. I sat in a massage
chair with my feet in a tub of warm
bubbling water. The mechanical fingers of
the chair wrenched the kinks in my back
giving me both pleasure and pain. When
she finished my feet, she rushed me to a
seat and dipped my fingers in warm water
then clipped away my dead skin. I went
with the more expensive gel polish, hoping
it would last longer, and a French manicure.
By the time she finished my toenails and
fingernails were so eye-catching they
looked as though they belonged to
someone else. I looked in the mirror and
saw a gorgeous young woman. For the first
time in days, since Einstein's death, joy
overcame me.

My physical makeover complete, I returned to the bus station and continued my journey to the airport. On the ride, I concluded my style of clothing needed a makeover too. I wore faded jeans, a T-shirt, and a heavy blue hoodie, hardly Justine glamor material. I needed dresses, skirts and fashionable sandals and boots.

At the airport I purchased my one-way ticket, which consisted of two stops - New York and Moscow, Russia - spending a grand total of thirty-three hours in flight. I had nothing but time, so I shopped, buying a couple elegant outfits before boarding. The airport wasn't any more confusing than the bus or train stations, although the security procedure was ridiculous and demeaning. I checked my bag and carried just my backpack, which I stuffed into a new, classier purse.

I hadn't flown in a plane and my stomach fluttered with anxiety. My mind envisioned an entire scenario: an unforeseen object crashing into us, causing a huge gap of twisted metal beneath our feet to open. It swallowed us and created a mass commotion among the passengers. People screamed and held onto seats or other objects to keep from being sucked into the oblivion and plummeting through the Earth's thick atmosphere to their deaths. I positioned my purse between my feet after takeoff, with a strap around my ankle in case my scenario rang true. When I plummeted to my death my pack was going with me, which I know, sounds silly, but my entire life, including important memories, were inside it.

The airline offered a meal, but it tasted disgusting, nothing like my cooking. For the price of a ticket, they should serve gourmet food. I lost my appetite. They showed a movie, but headphones cost four dollars. I took a headphone set when the man in the seat ahead of me sidetracked the flight attendant. The movie stunk, and I stuffed the headphones into the pocket sewn into the seat in front of me. Tendrils of warm fluid continued to rise and fall behind my eyes as memories of Einstein burned deep inside me.

I refocused myself and people watched. The man across from me ordered and drank seven tiny bottles of Chardonnay. A family sat kitty corner to my seat. The two older hellions bounced in their seats and down the aisles while the younger child sat quiet. The parents tried to scold the older two children, and they grew calmer, but then acted up when an opportunity arose. I sat next to a man who slept, snoring louder than the jet engine. His head, followed by his body, continued to slump onto me. I pushed him away from me, within minutes, he slumped back on me. A stocky woman barreled herself through the aisle and disappeared into the restroom just behind my seat. When she reappeared ten minutes later, so did a putrid odor, which nearly caused me to pass out. I forced my shirt over my mouth and nose, curling my face into my knees to suck in the fresh scent of my clothing.

Another person a couple rows in front of me kept talking on his phone and fiddling with his computer. Curious, I took a stroll to the restroom in front and attempted to sneak a quick glance. His coal eyes caught my look-see, and he closed the lid of his computer. Another passenger, his eyes shaking and bouncing, kept staring over his shoulder in my direction. I nicknamed him Mr. Dancy Eyes. My instincts or sixth sense kept me away from him. When the plane finally landed in Moscow, I was happy. I got off and stretched my legs even though I still had one more short flight.

I walked the entire airport during my layover stretching my cramped legs. My new identity and age made it possible for me to buy alcoholic beverages. A tall, thin man with a distinct case of male pattern baldness creeping across his head sat next to me at the bar, and asked, "Is this seat taken?"

"No."

"A beautiful lady like you traveling alone?"

My sixth sense told me to lie. "Yes, I'm meeting my fiancé in France."

His lips curled into a thin smile. "What a coincidence. I'm headed to Paris too. We have a couple hours, would you like another?"

"Thank you. So, what takes you to France?"

"We need to properly introduce ourselves. I'm Joe, and you are?" He took my hand and placed a kiss on it.

"Justine. Nice to meet you, Joe." I responded, regaining control of my hand.

"Well, Justine, it's a pleasure to meet you. I have business in Paris."

From the corner of my eye, I spotted Mr. Dancy Eyes from the plane, was it possible he was on his way to Paris too? I ignored his bouncing eyes which glared into my bare, broken hearted soul and continued my conversation with Joe accepting his drink offer. I drank slow and cautious, not wanting to get belligerent before boarding my last flight. It so happened Mr. Dancy Eyes was on my next flight too.

A New World

In Paris, I stepped into the fresh air and inhaled filling my lungs. Taxis and busses lined the roadways to carry people to their destinations. Without thought I boarded a bus headed towards a hotel, first checking to see if Mr. Dancy Eyes was around, I didn't see him. The bus dropped me off in front of a posh hotel, but I snuck off, not wanting a room yet. My legs needed to move after being scrunched in an airplane seat for several hours, and my belly rumbled from hunger.

I walked around Paris and took in the sights. The sun disappeared and evening settled upon the city. Paris was different to American cities I'd seen. The buildings and structures alluded they were older than time and added a mystical appeal to the city. Fewer cars littered the roads, many people walked, or rode bikes. The city was compact, opposite of American cities. I walked a few miles and stopped at a deli with outdoor seating. I opted to eat beneath the stars. Unable to read French, the waiter translated for me. My stomach betrayed my mind, I ate half the flatbread melt.

Einstein lingered in my thoughts and his caress as we first snuggled in the warehouse together. His arms holding me tight... pushing me out of the way, then his blank stare into my water filled eyes. I stood up, tears in the corners of my eyes, and threw money at the table as if it would catch the bills.

I needed a quiet place to gather my thoughts and collect myself. Not a cheap motel or abandoned building, but something grand like the hotel I first napped in after I left the shack. The name Justine commanded luxury beyond my wildest fantasies. Aimlessly, I ran smack into an extravagant, towering fairy tale palace hotel. Inside, glass chandeliers patched across the ceiling, and marble floors smoothed a path in front of me. Spinning in marvel, then floating in a slumber-like state I glided towards the counter.

With a thick French accent, the front desk man, his nametag read Jean, asked, "May I help you?"

"Yes, I need a room."

"Do you have a reservation?"

"A what?" I asked.

His eyebrows turned inward. "Reservation for a room. You must have one for us to place you."

My mind exploded. How stupid! I didn't understand reservations existed. I turned on my heels and walked towards the door without saying a word.

My ego deflated while bits and pieces of life with Einstein flashed through my head. From behind me a hand reached out and cradled my hand. A young man with light brown hair and deep brown velvety eyes stood opposite me. I met his eyes and peace washed through my soul. He explained a room was available and apologized for any inconvenience from the staff. He took my bags and helped me through the check-in process, then escorted me to a room on the fourth floor.

My eyes grew three sizes as I took in the room. The entire city twinkled in front of me through the opened curtains. Creams, gold, and shades of red completed the décor.

He pointed towards the mini bar. "Please help yourself free of charge, it's stocked." He walked to a cabinet and opened it revealing a TV. "If you need anything ask for me, Didier. I will make sure you are taken care of." He spoke American well, but the words rolled off his tongue with an alluring French accent.

Stunned, I searched to find the words, tears pooling in the corners of my eyes. "Thank you." I mustered in a near whisper.

After he left, I checked out the rest of the room. In the bathroom a basket filled with designer lotions, bubble baths, soaps, shampoos, conditioners, and deodorants sat on the marble counter. Towels wearing the hotel emblem hung in tidy triangles from a golden bar. I squeezed my hand around a towel, its softness and thickness squished between my fingers. The stocked mini bar contained liquors, wines and snacks. Juices, sodas, various foods, and several types of cheese lined the shelves of the refrigerator. I plopped on the bed. My butt sunk into the fluffy mattress and I feared I might disappear into it. I sprawled on the bed, spread my arms and legs like a snow angel and stared at the ceiling.

My mind and body focused on my lost love. *He would have liked this place.* I took out a picture of him and ran my finger across it as if I could touch him. Then I pulled a pillow to my face and cried into its creamy softness. Tears flowed for my lost friend, lover, and family member.

I forced myself to get up and bee-lined to the mini bar, grabbed a few of the small bottles of wine, and ran a steaming hot bubble bath. The bubbles came just below my ears, and I sank into their effervescence as I drank and thought. I needed to know more about Einstein; where had he come from? Who was he? Who was Justine Holmes? That decision was mine. I needed to make an identity for her, bring her to life. My new life would be everything my other life hadn't been, and I would live in the lap of luxury. After drinking the few small bottles of wine, I grew happy and excited about my new life. I would put my past behind me. The only exception was finding more about my beloved Einstein.

After the bath I wrapped myself in a creamy-soft towel and melted underneath it. I meandered over to the mini bar again and grabbed a bottle of clear liquor with a vanilla scent. I pulled off the top and swallowed the contents of the bottle. Ewww! I chocked and gagged involuntarily. My mouth and throat were on fire, and the heat sank to my stomach, which burned. The room spun around me, and I fell against something soft.

I awoke with a pounding headache, reached for the absent covers, pried my eyes open, and attempted to focus. As my eyes adjusted, I saw a wooden table leg staring back at me, a strong hint I was lying on the plush carpet. My body didn't want to move, so I lay there staring at the ceiling. I remembered where and who I was as my eyes acclimated to my surroundings.

Through the curtains, the bright morning sun filled the sky. At the bar sat a small coffee pot, bags of coffee, and a plate of pastries. I had no memory of the pastries from the previous night. What time did I pass out? What time was it now?

I reached in my bag, and pulled out Einstein's wristwatch, it displayed seven fifteen, Friday morning. My plane arrived Wednesday evening, I settled in the room that night, now it was Friday? I remembered synching his watch to Paris time upon my arrival which meant I slept over twenty-four hours. Never in my life... I let it go as caused by jet lag.

I made a pot of coffee and devoured the delicious pastries while contemplating how best to find information on Einstein. By nine thirty I headed towards the lobby, showered, dressed, and with an idea. I asked the concierge for an international paper, assuming the global news was a good starting place for my research. The concierge, Jean the same man from Wednesday, presented a paper, which I accepted. I caught the elevator back up to my room; the ride was smooth and silent.

I read and read but found nothing mentioning a hit and run in small-town Alabama, maybe the hotel had guest computers. Einstein the computer whiz taught me how to surf the net. I journeyed back to the lobby and asked Jean.

"Does the hotel have guest computers?"

"Non." He grabbed a crude map off a clear display rack and directed me to a café a few blocks from the hotel.

In the café I searched the net, looking for recent deaths, hit and runs, murders, and accidental deaths. Nothing! I typed *Alabama newspapers* in the search bar. Bingo, there it was. Now I had a starting point! I looked through recent articles and found it. *Young man hit by car... driver fled scene… mysterious 911 call… thought to be driver… young woman.*

I continued reading and searching, *The young man identified as Burke Childrone… reported missing. His parents, owners of Childrone Publishing, flew into town to take his body… detectives worked around the clock.* My mind spun. His name was Burke, and he came from a wealthy family. Why did he leave? Did he leave of his own accord? Why else would he leave? Answers, and new questions. I continued to search for missing persons. An investigation followed his disappearance. His parents hired detectives to find their son. At one point the police suspected his parents of foul play. No evidence against them surfaced, so the police took them off the suspect list. Einstein, or Burke, disappeared into thin air. He left for school in the morning and never returned home. The police and his family presumed him dead. I knew the truth. He blended into the streets filled with runaways.

A French woman with stern eyes interrupted my research when she walked to my table and pointed towards the clock. My cue the café was closing, and I needed to leave. I gathered my notes and left.

Evening settled, and a wave of brilliant lights moved across the city.

As I strolled to the hotel an overwhelming sensation that someone was following me flooded my soul, and hunger pains gripped my stomach. I attempted to reason that my new knowledge clouded my judgement, but my sixth sense told me different. A café to my right offered a place to evaluate my surroundings, regroup, and eat. It wasn't wise to continue my journey to the hotel with a spy following me. I took a seat outside and glanced over the menu, everything looked delicious. I ordered *the special*, a Parisian meat pie. It turned out to be tasty. As a homeless runaway I learned to live off the land, so to speak, meaning dumpsters, teaching me not to be picky.

I scanned the surroundings and spied a man with a bald patch on top his head standing beneath a tree a few yards from me. Mr. Dancy Eyes? Was it the same man, or my imagination going wild? His eyes bounced like a dime machine ball and he refused to look directly at me. Would someone follow me here to arrest me for my crimes? Could they arrest me on foreign soil? I didn't know the answer to any of my questions and didn't think it a coincidence he stood within eyeshot of me. Soon as I finished my meal, I threw money on the table and left.

Jumpin' Pumpkins!

I walked and walked ducking through alleys and shops attempting to confuse and lose him. When I no longer felt the sting of his bouncing eyes on my back I headed to the hotel. I spent so much mental energy evading him I'd gotten lost then I remembered the crude map Jean gave me; I unfolded it, checked street signs, and plotted the course. When I reached the hotel, I wound my way up to my room, dropped on my bed and thought of my discoveries.

Ring! Ring! The phone blasted and my body jumped in an involuntary lurch, falling off the bed. I scrambled to my feet, and picked up the phone, as if it would blow up in my hands.

"Hello?"

"Miss Holmes, this is Didier. How is your stay?" His French accent melted the words off his tongue, and my anxiety disappeared.

"I'm great, and yes, all my needs are met."

"If there is anything more I can do to make your stay unforgettable, don't hesitate to ask." Is it customary for hotel owners to call their guests?

"Thank you." I placed the phone on the receiver.

Within minutes of hanging up the phone a knock rattled the door. Room service? I hadn't placed an order. I grabbed a doll sized statue seated on a table, in case Mr. Dancy Eyes stood on the other side, and opened the door. To my thankful surprise it wasn't Mr. Dancy Eyes, but a bottle of complimentary wine and a bouquet. The delivery boys' eyes scanned the statue in my hands, and he pushed the gifts toward me as if to block my blow. With a sheepish grin I set the statue back on the table and took the vase and wine. A card on a stick hidden amongst the flowers read *Invitation*. I opened it and read, *Join me at the restaurant downstairs for dinner under the stars tomorrow, Didier* with a yes and no box underneath the print. The boy handed me a pen. I marked the yes box and gave it to him. After all, now I was glamorous Justine, and lived an exquisite life. He nodded as he caught it by the corner then scurried to the elevator.

I spent the following day shopping for glamorous Justine clothing and date material – sexy and beguiling. Stylish clothing stores littered Paris, which oddly gave me a hidden sense of security while shopping for dresses and designer shoes. My lesson for the day was understanding the difference between designer names and knockoffs. The never-ending assortment of fashions included something for everyone's taste. I bought an eye-catching green knock-off dress that my budget allowed. The front came down in a V across my chest displaying the round curves of my breasts beneath and the back fell in long, shallow layers. It was alluring and most definitely Justine.

I met Didier at the hotel restaurant as the note instructed. We ate dinner while the wine flowed. Charm surged from every word Didier spoke. His dark brown hair fell below his ears with thick waves scattering across his head, green halos surrounded his coffee-colored eyes. I'm sure he had no shortage of women chasing him and wondered what he saw in me.

I wanted to be in the present with him but my mind raced to the reason I was in Paris, Einstein. Memories of him swarmed through my mind. By contrast, his straight blond hair hung long with split ends frizzing the bottom from lack of a good haircut, most often he wore it tied back. Deep solid dark chocolate wide eyes sat the perfect distance from his nose, and his build tall and lean. Didier was at least three inches shorter with muscles exploding beneath his shirt sleeves, and a couple years older, my guess early twenties. After dinner we walked around Paris. Romance blossomed from every inch of the city blooming into vibrant flowers of passion.

Didier told life stories, and I weaved a lie about growing up in Texas. I made up the life I wished I'd lived because it would be easier to remember such a lie. About Einstein I was honest without giving more details than necessary. "My boyfriend passed away, a car wreck. That's why I'm here, it's been difficult, and I needed to get away." I dammed up the river waiting to gush behind my eyes.

The sympathy in his voice gave away his genuine concern. "We'll work on that. There is much to see here, and if you'll allow me, I will show it all to you." The breeze rustled the leaves on the surrounding trees creating music which sang to my ears – freedom and a fresh beginning.

Over the next few days we spent a lot of time together sight-seeing. The Didier tour of Paris. He adored art and took me to the Musée Picasso and Musée d'Orsay. I admired the art and the hand that painted it, however, most of it didn't make sense to me, although I didn't express that to him. Instead, I encouraged him to teach me lessons about the art.

He took me to the Eiffel Tower, Notre-Dame, and we went to Les Catacombs, tunnels and tunnels of dead people, spooky. We went to Parc Floral, one of the most stunning sights I had seen in my entire life, color and sweet aromas exploded from every angle. French people celebrated death and life and admired art and fine wine. The longer I stayed the more in love with Paris I grew. Nothing appeared real leading to the pseudo-perception that Justine was untouchable melting into the atmosphere and mystery that shrouded Paris.

After a week of wining and dining, Didier stole my breath away. He took me to a penthouse room in his hotel, blues and creams popped from the décor while silks and velvets covered the windows and furniture. The fluffy carpet squished beneath my feet, and the room was large enough it took up half the space on the top floor. Thin cream sheers held up at the corners with gold pins surrounded the bed. A massive entertainment system with items I didn't understand what they were or how to work them sat to the right of the bed. In the center of the huge room two blue velvet chaise lounges faced the entertainment center with a small table tucked between them. A two-burner stove, full size refrigerator, and breakfast bar completed the kitchenette. Long blue velvet curtains held up with gold rings covered the large picture windows puddling on the floor beneath them. A wrought iron chair was visible between the cracks in the curtains.

I padded to the curtains and pushed them aside revealing a twin wrought iron chair and small round table. The terrace extended longer than the length of the room, overlapped the next room, a small gate separated the areas. The entire city twinkled before my eyes while my mouth dropped to my feet in awe. I opened the door and took a seat allowing myself to dissolve into the breathtaking view. A few weeks ago, I couldn't have imagined being in a room this elegant, much less dating its owner.

From behind, Didier wrapped his arms around me, his mouth caressed my cheek kissing it softly, startling me. He zapped away my loneliness in that single moment, I no longer felt like a paper character in a fictional book. His gentle kisses danced across my neck, leaving a warm patch that sent tingles through my spine. I hoped this wonderful dream would last an eternity.

"How do you like the room?" He asked in his silky voice.

"It's more beautiful than any room I've ever seen."

His mouth widened into a smile. "Good, this is your room to stay in as long as you are in Paris. You don't need to worry about anything; it's all taken care of."

The poetic way he said it played a melody in my ears. The dam now opened wide, and a river of tears streamed from my eyes. Could I live here in this luxury? I was nobody, a girl who came from a small shack with no hot water! I lived on the streets and ate trash! He knew none of this, just the tale I wove - the life of Justine, not Cleo, or my alter ego before Cleo. I stood up, turned towards Didier, wrapped my arms around his neck, perched on my tiptoes, and whispered, "Thank you" in his ear. I refused to turn away such luxurious living accommodations when I had no income, and from such an exhilarating man.

He wiped the tears below my eyes. "Why do you cry?"

"Your generosity."

He folded me into his arms and kissed my lips, his tongue playing tangle games with mine. Warmth radiated through my body and the word "love" came to mind.

www.ingramcontent.com/pod-product-compliance
Lightning Source LLC
Chambersburg PA
CBHW032049180726
48284CB00004B/1259